Where Skies Are Not Cloudy

Where Skies Are Not Cloudy

Walter McDonald

University of North Texas Press

© 1993 by Walter McDonald

10 9 8 7 6 5 4 3 2 1

Requests for permission to reproduce material from
this work should be sent to:

Permissions
University of North Texas Press
Post Office Box 13856
Denton, Texas 76203

Texas Poets Series Number 4

The paper in this book meets the minimum requirements of the American
National Standard for Permanence of Paper for Printed Library materials,
z39.48-1984.

Library of Congress Cataloging-in-Publication Data

McDonald, Walter.
    Where skies are not cloudy / Walter McDonald.
        p.   cm. — (Texas poets series : #4)
    ISBN 0-929398-61-0 (cloth) : ISBN 0-929398-60-2 (paper)
    I. Title. II. Series: Texas poets series ; v. 4.
PS3563.A2914W48   1993
811'.54—dc20   93-14496
                                                        CIP

ACKNOWLEDGMENTS

I'm grateful to the following publication in which these poems first appeared, some with different titles.

Agni: "After Eden"
American Literary Review: "All Boys Are Humpty Dumpty"; "The Barn on the Brazos"; "Something Simple Like the Weather"
Ariel (Canada): "All the Old Songs"
Art/Life: "Uncle Leland and the Boulders"
Berkeley Poetry Review: "Pets on the Farm"
Cincinnati Poetry Review: "The Last Good Saddles"
Clockwatch Review: "In the Hibiscus Garden"
College English: "Hawks in the World They Own"; "The Skulls that Eat such Dust"
Colorado Review: "War in the Persian Gulf"
Country Journal: "Calves Swaggering on Stilts"
Creeping Bent: "The Southern Brown Recluse"
CutBank: "Bait"
Fiddlehead (Canada): "Steeples and Deep Wells"
Fine Madness: "The War Years"
Florida Review: "Whatever Our Fists Find"
Georgia Review: "Great Expectations"
G.W. Review: "Father's Shotgun"
Images: "We Will All Live on the Plains"
Journal of American Culture: "Black Granite Burns Like Ice"
Kansas Quarterly: "Following Instinct and Cactus"
Manoa: "The Summer before the War"
Maryland Poetry Review: "Picasso and the Art of Angels"
Mississippi Valley Review: "Memorial Day"; "Thrusting from Earth Inverted"
Missouri Review: "In Green Pastures"; "Uncle Roy's Pearl Harbor Hot Dogs"
Nebraska Review: "Summer Nights"
New Letters: "Learning to Aim Well"
New Mexico Humanities Review: "Homecoming, Class of '52"
New Review: "Across Dark Fields of Coyotes"
New Texas 92: "Billy Joe's Roadside Museum"
New Virginia Review: "Where Skies Are Not Cloudy All Day"
North American Review: "Found in an Alley Dumpster"
North Dakota Quarterly: "Faith Is a Radical Master"; "Frogs Croaking Their Love Songs"; "Mending the Fence"
Ohio Review: "No Matter Where We've Been"
Oxford Magazine: "Releasing the Hawk in August"

Pacific Review: "In Gusty Winds This Wild"
Panhandler: "Macho"
Poet & Critic: "The Laws of Hollow Wings"
Poet Lore: "Falling in Love over Dallas"
Poetry Durham (U.K.): "Goats Imported from Austin"
Poetry Northwest: "Dawn of the Bitter Blizzard"
Poetry Wales (U.K.): "A Thousand Yards Downhill"
Raccoon: "After Watching the Space Shuttle Explode"
Sewanee Review: "In Fields of Buffalo"
Shenandoah: "When the Circus Is Over"
Soundings East: "Nearing the End of a Century"
Southern Poetry Review: "'How Did I Get so Old?'"
Three Rivers Poetry Journal: "Sunday Morning Roundup"
University of Windsor Review (Canada): "Dog-Day Afternoon"
Widener Review: "A Stroll Around the Dance Floor"

"The Skulls that Eat such Dust," and "Hawks in the World They Own"
copyright ©1988, 1992 by the National Council of Teachers of English.
Reprinted by permission of the publisher. Parts of "The Skulls that Eat
such Dust" were published in *Santa Clara Review*.
"In Fields of Buffalo" was published in *The Sewanee Review* (volume 101,
number 1, Winter 1993). Copyright 1993 by Walter McDonald.

I'm especially grateful to the National Endowment for the Arts and to Texas
Tech University for time to write many of these poems.

CONTENTS

4. Dawn of the Bitter Blizzard

5. Across Dark Fields of Coyotes

1.

No Matter Where We've Been

IN GREEN PASTURES

Now it begins, oaks spinning winter
into leaves. Oiling the windmill blades,
I back to the edge and watch them spin.
Out pumps the same sweet water

from the pipe. Bracing with one stiff hand,
I squirt another drop for luck
and grab the ladder, swing out one leg
and glance around—the flat backs of Herefords

trudging to the trough, trees dense
as a windbreak, the glint of neighbors' roofs.
Without a breeze, we'd all
be stranded without a gourd of water.

We take beguiling skies for granted
on the plains, the hands we hold from habit.
Most hours, we ignore the clatter of steel,
the mystery of wells, each other's

steady breath. Tonight, we'll rock
on the porch swing, hearing the bawl
of a calf, a dog barking a mile away,
the whirring blades.

HAWKS IN THE WORLD THEY OWN

Rattlers choking down rabbits
are mascots of our eyes. In saddles,
we pause and watch the show, the snake
all jaw, swallowing the rabbit whole,

more glutton than steers which chew
their stubble twice. Hawks glide
blue skies in spite of drought.
Steers roam the fields heads down,

praying to only grass. We ride the range
for signs, hoping for more than rain.
We can't root out all cactus in pastures
made for rattlesnakes and goats. Our eyes

unlock like jaws and swallow all we see.
A hawk needs nothing on a ranch we own.
Our rifles are threats he ignores,
steel wands directing traffic of coyotes.

Hawks go their own way, alone,
believing the wind sustains them,
the sun was made for their wings only,
the world has endless rabbits.

NO MATTER WHERE WE'VE BEEN

I swore I'd never come back
to the plains, eighty flat acres
and stars so bright they buzzed.

I said I'd work these rows only for sport,
maize for a pair of calves.
Goats and hawks are hobbies, a creek

with bass once in a hundred casts.
Old Uncle Bubba told me
no matter where we've been,

it's home. Our boys make a fortune
dragging home rattlers in towsacks.
The prairie crawls with tarantulas,

hawks in all weather.
There's little we could lose, here,
little we could hide.

We've almost stopped pretending
clouds are mountains.
If we can't accept these fields,

our own souls with all their wind
and cactus, we ought to leave.
Even at night, our shadows sprawl:

this moon is up for hours. On fields
this flat, someone's easy to find
and always calls us friend.

THRUSTING FROM EARTH INVERTED

Often I've caught a glint of silver,
pilots trusting their dials and turbines.
Odd, walking flat fields after years
in a cockpit, caught between the earth
and angels. How many loops and barrel rolls,
thrusting from earth inverted, how many dives

and pull-outs, straining to stop blood
rushing from my skull. I see young pilots
on TV, faces lined from their masks,
cropped hair and ancient eyes,
the stance of tigers. I remember Millard
and Roy Carnes shot down in jungle,

Bob Ross and Jones, and Billy Ray Moegle,
the squadron clown, dragged through Hanoi,
still missing—boys on fire with laughter,
who thought God was on our side
through any skies we dared,
the future paved with runways leading home.

STEEPLES AND DEEP WELLS

No sense of guilt: that must be
what they sought, driving bull-necked oxen
to the plains, teams stubborn as mules
grazing swaying grass knee-deep all day,

wagons stranded like crippled buffalo
a thousand miles from Kentucky loam
and lakes, pleasures of the flesh
where sin came easy. Here they found no trees,

no stones to hide behind. If any came blameless,
here their faults were plain.
No wonder they shoveled dug-outs first,
somewhere to sleep out of sight.

On land so flat they dug deep wells
and raised plank steeples fast,
as lightning rods. If they wondered
about chances left behind, the sun

burned the truth of what they were,
one crop away from being meat for buzzards.
Rain fell like manna and saved
their starving crops. Believing signs

of planted trees all winter,
they doled out grain and shivered.
They shared their meager fields with hawks
and ate the flesh of wolves.

FROGS CROAKING THEIR LOVE SONGS

At dusk we visit neighbors we've ignored.
We miss good friends and children who've moved away.
Let wishes keep all friends alive. Hold on,

we call, we're coming. The sun comes up
and nothing's changed. Our hands were made
for teats and milk cans, the daily rations

for cows lined up and bawling. Cows waddle off
to graze, to dream of bulls. I slam the gate
and latch it, stomping my boots to clean them.

We tell a prairie all we hope it means,
inventing corrals and barns. Each year,
we bulldoze tons of weedy mesquites

and stack the roots, another acre for pasture.
All day, we whisper nothing. The loudest shouts
are lost on steers and goats that ignore us.

We hold communion with wheat and oats,
no end to feeding. Goats butt the troughs,
shoving each other off, hooking their horns

like uncles wrangling on the county square,
wagging goatees and coughing. We watch dark wings
forever gliding, skies never at a loss for hawks.

At night, we listen to the splash of bass in the pond,
frogs croaking their love songs, millions of stars
lighting their leaps to each other. At dawn,

we sit outside and watch the stars go under,
each blink of our eyes erasing thousands,
the sun slower than us but coming.

MENDING THE FENCE

I twist the barbed wire tight
to hold the dumbest cow. Another rip,
these gloves no older than wires I strung
last year, already sagging.

Whirlwinds are devils roaming the fields
for mischief. Something shoves posts down
and makes good neighbors strangers—
hunters mad at the moon

shooting at shadows, cows straining
through barbed wires, a pack of dogs
at night, flung back by wires,
losing the track of a rabbit.

I've seen them sometimes in shadows,
stray pets becoming wolves.
Caught in the pickup's headlights, they blink
and slink away through cactus,

flashing their tails in moonlight.
I've found cows bloodied, necks caught
by barbed wires, walleyed and bawling,
their fat tongues purple.

I wave to anyone on horseback
or walking across my pasture
under a sky of buzzards. If he's alone,
if I haven't heard a shot for hours,

I let him go, hoping I'll find
no fence posts broken,
no cow gut-shot and bleeding,
her wild eyes staring at heaven.

LEARNING TO AIM WELL

Where they fall,
    doves scatter dust,
        wings sweeping like brooms.

They twitch,
    bleeding muddy beads
        like pearls.

Boys the first time out
    lean back.
        Their spit tastes brown.

Fathers pinch off the heads
    like licorice.
        The doves kick once.

Boys quiver,
    looking down. Their doves
        seem more like birds

than those their fathers shot
    dead center, eyes closed,
        perfect pearl-gray trophies.

SUNDAY MORNING ROUNDUP

I guide my sorrel down a steep arroyo,
cursing each crumbling step of shale, oil-rich,
if I could afford to drill it.
I tell my mama's conscience

work is a virtue of godly men on Sunday
when starving bobcats believe spring calves
are born to feed them. Better here
than in some high-roofed church with robed choirs

shouting Latin. I've hummed this hymn a thousand times
and mean it, washed by the blood of the Lamb,
though I can't stand mutton. Red meat for me,
cattle and goats the only hoofs I'd have

on prairies fit for scorpions. I let the gelding
climb back to the plains, following the dog,
nothing in that valley of shadows
but bones, not one spiralling buzzard in sight

and it's almost noon, time to stumble on a big cat
sleeping it off, feeling smug as a rich man
counting his barns. The dog stops and stiffens,
wants to bay but doesn't, breaks running

toward a weed-grown playa lake. Tapping the reins,
I gallop toward shadow, a flash of weeds,
and tug my Stetson tight against the wind,
lean down and slide the rifle out.

CALVES SWAGGERING ON STILTS

Cows fall in love with each other,
a pasture of calves more urgent
than grass. Under an oak,
I watch them beating time
with horns and swishing tails.

They mount, they bellow love
for the world, afraid of nothing.
Bring on the bulls, they say,
chewing their cud and swaying.
All week, I lead cows to the stall,

the ceremony. Trucked back,
turned out to pasture,
they drop their bone heads down
to whatever's spread before them,
hunger like steel rings

leading them by the nose, the slow
piling up of boredom, all grass alike,
made for their tongues only.
They give themselves to prayer,
head-down and grazing. Their bodies

repeat the mystery, turning grass to milk.
Good mothers, they stand all summer
and let calves beat their udders
like punching bags, all they can drink.
Calves swagger off on awkward stilts

as if they own the world,
a pasture of cows and salt blocks,
ignoring the fattened steers,
the cattle trucks,
the bulls in steel-post stalls.

2.

Summer Nights

SUMMER NIGHTS

We listened to voices ringing on the rails,
swapped rumors of girls and babies,
wars our uncles fought, weapons and scalps
hidden in attics. Trapped on the plains,
we shared flat cactus fields with coyotes

then tried to shoot them. They knew us
and kept their distance, complaining to the moon.
We shoved our boots into bedrolls
on the same cool sand with rattlers.
Billy Joe swore he heard one in jostled pods

of a yucca. We wondered what bumped it,
werewolves or ghosts we believed in
under a moon that full, our wide eyes
watching mesquite trees like witches
waving a thousand arms.

IN FIELDS OF BUFFALO

Granddaddy waited while men with spades
dug a maze of trenches to test the treasure maps.
Skulls wedged up like onions on his farm.
Diggers from Austin brought along charts
of slaughter on the plains. By 1880,

buffalo hunters had aimed long rifles
where he plowed. Thousands dropped like manna
for horseflies, hides worth their weight
in silver in St. Louis. . . . I remember the truck,
the loading ramp, crates of bones dollied aboard.

I hadn't known buffalo roamed there,
never dreamed his dirt was home to anyone
before Grandfather's father. Cotton
was all I'd seen on his rows, those skies
my only horizon. At night I listened hard

and heard far in the distance the howl of coyotes,
the thunder of summer storms. Lying still,
I felt an earthquake rumble, a herd
stampeded by rifles, miles of humpbacks
galloping, about to disappear.

BAIT

Behind the barn, we trapped crawdads
in the creek Granddaddy used for bait.
Catfish in the Brazos a mile away
ignored us, old whiskers floating.

The ones we wanted lay in shade
on the bottom like lazy bulls.
Fish Granddaddy caught on trotlines
weighed more than us, their oily,

leather lips wide as our skulls.
And so, after we roped ourselves
as anchors to the nearest trees,
we rigged broom handles with bailing wire

twisted to hooks. Skewered crawdads
made the perfect bait. They squished
as big hooks punctured them. Dangled,
they writhed like fat pale spiders.

We held them squirming and stared,
then heaved them into the brown, muddy Brazos,
feet set against the explosion of hunger,
the appearance of things not seen.

GOATS IMPORTED FROM AUSTIN

Goats stumbled on shale, a rocky mesa
Daddy fenced for kids imported from Austin.
He swore *cabrito* would be worth the smell,
a market killing, but hated goats—

cattle the only odor for a man. Coyotes and rattlers
roamed those acres until he claimed them.
Goats climbed the hill like big-horn sheep,
playing king of the mountain, bold on the bluff,

staring at greener pastures. Other goats popped up
like penguins, searching for all he saw in the distance.
My brother and I fed goats by hand, lugged oats
to kids with nubbin horns, bellies that bulged

and muscles butting us for buckets. After chores,
we dragged our wagons to the top. Where the cliff
dropped off, we risked the bumpy ride downhill,
tumbling, bending the wheels and tongues.

The goats ignored us, picking their paths
up and down like angels. After frost,
our father slaughtered them all and hung them
one by one from rafters, smoking the meat

for winter, the market for cattle and goats
collapsed, the start of the Texas depression.
Drinking windmill water to swallow,
we chewed tough jerky for years,

salt-cured and stringy. We learned to curse
the dust of a ranch that failed
and played field hockey without a stick,
kicking the tiny hoofs like pucks.

UNCLE ROY'S PEARL HARBOR HOT DOGS

Uncle Roy wore American flags
for a topcoat, a hat made of owls'
and eagles' feathers. Ringing a bell downtown
he rolled an oblong hot-dog cart
shaped like a bomb in World War II.

He daubed white stripes and stars
gaudy and rippling. He bent the tin
and fastened it with screws,
live coals inside to warm the meat and buns.
Before the war, he had pedaled around

without a family, one eye wobbling
in traffic, the other laughing.
He waved at anyone, and most of us
waved back, uncle to all in name only.
After Pearl Harbor, we saw him on foot

dragging scraps of tin into alleys.
One day there he came, big bomb of hot dogs
and Uncle Roy in flags, calling, "Dogs!
Beat Hitler with a dog!" Who taught him
what to charge we never learned,

maybe angels he heard on Sundays—a dime
for himself, a dime for war bonds.
Wheels wobbled under the load
as he shoved our daily food downtown,
ringing, ringing the bell.

THE WAR YEARS

Even the sniff of a cork
made him stagger, a sip of muscatel
or eggnog-whiskey at Christmas.
My aunts grumbled, why did she
keep going out at night

and hauling him home like trash,
staggering like a bear rug
over her on the porch, singing
and shouting louder than alley cats.
My sister and I hid in our fists

till it was over.
When the house was dark
Mother leaned down and touched us
like a ghost. Our father
dried out like a pillar of salt

when I was six, the year our oldest brother
burned in the Pacific, the night
a kamikaze crashed amidships
where our brother manned the pumps.
For years, our father went to work,

came home and said hello
and sat alone on the back porch
rocking, sipping cold coffee,
holding that black and gold photo,
looking back.

UNCLE LELAND AND THE BOULDERS

Uncle Leland saved drivers from landslides,
sun-burned on a tilting bulldozer. Boulders
rubbled his talk, a torrent of curses
boys like me believed in more than his pictures
of switchbacks. He swore the plains
where I grew up were mountains pounded flat.
His cigar spasmed ashes on the floor,

this uncle who rescued me from boredom at fourteen.
After childless Aunt Norma died, he came home
twice a year to my mother, his only sister.
I worshipped his muscles and savage tattoos.
He taught me tricks of friction with baseballs,
the fulcrum of wrestling, the odds of balance
and how to fall. Drunk, he pounded the walls

and wept about bad jokes of boulders crashing down
whenever his back was turned. How could a boy
stop whatever tumbled down in a fit of coughing?
Wrecks rusting below bore witness to carving
mountains without a net. Others he saved daily
with a blade and throttle, but couldn't save
a wife who only wanted babies.

On plains I couldn't wait to leave,
he cursed stones wedged in the back of mountains,
risking the slope to shove them tumbling.
I felt his mountains shudder, his bulldozer tilt
and rumble, belching diesel, gnashing into reverse
to back off and drop the blade,
roaring once more toward the edge.

FALLING IN LOVE OVER DALLAS

Acres of rouged, good-hearted girls
rolled cream cones on their tongues.
Strolling the fairgrounds, they swayed away
from our tight Levis. Boys who rode bulls,

we'd come to see blue-ribbon heifers,
stallions, cattle the size of barns.
Under stars darkened by carnival lights,
barkers paraded women with veils

and cellulite. We'd never seen dancers
old as our mothers, grinding plump dimpled hips.
Tracks slammed us down like bulls we rode back home.
We crashed daredevil cars and dived on roller coasters.

We followed three saucy girls up the sky-jump,
who waved under billowing skirts. From the top,
we watched their parachutes touch down.
Our hearts dropped, caught by cables

far too slow. Under our shiny, dangling boots,
those fancy girls walked off and left us
tethered on hooks over Dallas, begging their names,
falling in love and waving, jerking the wires.

THE SUMMER BEFORE THE WAR

Fist like velcro on the rope,
Billy Ray nodded and the gate exploded,
mad bull kicking and heaving. How many times
did bones limber as bows take the shock
of falls, two local boys before Saigon,
waltzing with blondes in Saturday night cafés.
Old songs keep scrolling back on TV sales,
CD's or tapes like war videos

no one but fools like us would order.
What we longed for wasn't caught on film,
unwritten lyrics on our tongues.
Nights come back like taps to haunt us
privately, not boldly like a rodeo
where all could watch how well we rode,
how badly, which bulls we stayed on,
which ones stomped us hard.

THE LAWS OF HOLLOW WINGS

Wired to a plastic plug, I corkscrewed
up at the sun, alone in a jet at last.
Centuries led me to this, men who dreamed of wings
and walked on cobblestones—the Wrights
at Kitty Hawk, da Vinci's diagrams.

Fist tight on the throttle, I practiced dives
and lazy eights, wingovers and perfect rolls.
That bird was mine, ten thousand pounds of thrust.
Tips balanced on horizons, I looped the world
with only my fists to save me. Over the top,

my wings bumped in airspeed building fast
in the pullout. Level, I saw the field
where Roland crashed the week before,
the wreckage mangled, charred beyond belief.
He must have dived hypoxic, wobbling,

and tried to land, for the wheels were down.
What did he feel in those last seconds—the earth,
as he tried to flare, not flat at all,
but rows flicking by like strobe lights,
his last call garbled gasps.

3.
Faith Is a Radical Master

AFTER EDEN

Goats nuzzled all we own, stubble and grain.
We seeded sandy pastures and ordered bees by mail.
Praying for rain, who could believe in clouds?
All night we heard the moan of pistons,

the suck and clatter of sump pumps.
All neighbors' basements floated.
Crazed weather dumped such floods
on plains where rain is a miser.

Who buys dry acres risks more than rattlesnakes—
cactus and scrub mesquite the certain crops.
All week, we left our windows wide
and kicked the sheets, hoping for a breeze,

for no more rain. We sang sea chanties gladly
and kept the children home. Our dogs
sloshed through the yard, barking at rattlers
thrashing madly for an ark.

NEARING THE END OF A CENTURY

My great-greats claimed these acres,
trying to turn back bull-necked oxen
grazing prairie grass. From a dugout,
they watched fires burn the plains. Now,

the prairie is tamed, crack houses rampant,
the smoke of fire storms. Lot's wife has company,
enough salt columns to prop the ozone.
Aliens with outrageous smiles

ring our doorbell, burning to save the whale,
the elephant. Downtown, old men have given up,
their cardboard huts collapsed. Strangers
with signs picket all busy intersections.

I tell my sons don't look away. In Jericho
the spies made friends with Rahab,
the one whore laughing at the guards.
I think of Jonah watching the whale rise slowly

from the ocean, the startled sea gulls screeching.
Can deserts like dead bones live?
The Philistines gloated over blinded Samson
groaning, and heard the marble columns crack.

BILLY JOE'S ROADSIDE MUSEUM

The door slammed shut, a haunted house
of beasts and rodents mounted by amateurs,
a mail-order course in taxidermy.
Cobras old and dusty sagged over us.

We ducked under a vine
hung like a cord for a doorbell. *Is Tarzan in?*
Is Cheetah? Under dead eyes of lions
and fangs of tigers, we shuffled single file,

gullible game for the owner.
One stuffed gorilla bared Styrofoam teeth,
his shaggy arms propped out by wires.
Dried paint like blood stuck to his lips,

his leather chest. What fools,
a thousand miles to go and there we were
in catacombs of buffalo and vipers,
a jumble of snakes and bobcats,

the dusty heads of bucks and javelinas.
Buzzards hunched above on our way out.
I wanted those birds to turn,
their wattles to wobble, to clack their beaks

and wink. Even rattlesnakes ignored us
at the door, mounted on tables of sand,
only their fangs and rattles real,
black plastic for their eyes.

PICASSO AND THE ART OF ANGELS

The day Picasso died,
he dreamed he saw an angel
and wept he could never paint her,
marvelously complex,

the skin tones perfect,
her flesh angelically erotic,
nothing at all like humans,
the skewed, cubistic angles

of the actual. Did he know
as he reached for his brushes,
watching her hands fold towels
as if to drape herself

inside a perfect canvas,
did he know she was only
his morning nurse, a local woman
working for pay?

FOUND IN AN ALLEY DUMPSTER

Bury the sack, and let more cats
make kittens. Only a fool
would kill blind kittens
with a stone. But here they are,
carved out of fur and blood,

their teeth like zippers
that won't close. Whoever bashed
and tossed them in our dumpster
had in mind silence, the fastest
way to fix unwanted cats

simply to beat them with a brick
like crushing ice. Their blood
is crusted, their eyes
shut tight. We're sure
they never saw a human face.

ALL BOYS ARE HUMPTY DUMPTY

With cigars and balding heads
my brothers joke and make the old lies bolder,
fist fights and easy girls we loved.

They've kidded me for years, teasing
I'm the baby, forever the scapegoat.
They laugh at their clumsy brother

who tumbled from a fence to the pigpen,
walleyed, out of breath, pigs fumbling
and shoving above me, a herd of shoats

and me the cliff they charged.
Thumped down in the dust and pig dung,
I heard grunts and felt hot devil snouts

rooting my face and crotch.
I remember my brothers shouting,
the whack of sticks casting out demons,

pigs squealing and stumbling
in sunlight and dust
and someone lifting me.

MACHO

Crawling between mesquite and cactus,
I hold my rifle low
so the sun won't strike it.

Downwind from the only buck I've seen
in weeks, I rise up slowly for a shot,
hoping the hawks won't spook him.

But he's gone, hiding in brush
or leaping down steep arroyos.
This is how it is some days,

crawl on your belly like a snake,
taking nothing home but dust,
picking burrs from your shirt,

hard work like love, labor we live on
after sundown. What if the sun
was never a god, a burning bush,

a chariot? Could it be swamp gas,
boots, perpetual stutter?
Or the rich man's tongue in torment

with only the moon's eclipse
like a finger dipped in water to cool it?
More like a man after all?

PETS ON THE FARM

Bury the cow and let stray cats
go begging. Mice in the barn
can feed them, if they'll stop dozing,
mewing for their daily milk

arched warm and streaming
between their teeth. Let them lap
cold milk from a carton.
That's the last cow

I'll let our children beg
and raise as a heifer.
No more lugging bales of straw,
no more maize to pour in a trough,

no cloud of grain-dust to cough.
I'll sleep past five if I want to
without teats to clean with a sponge.
I'll ride my horse at sunset

around an empty pasture
past another hump of dirt
that will settle, after rains.
Let coyotes inherit salt blocks

scattered in clover,
let mice have all the grain
they find tied up in towsacks,
more mice for the cats.

Cats are the right pets for a farm,
something we don't have to feed
or care about or bury.
I'm through with the chores

and raw milk of childhood,
the care of stalling calves
for children who weep so easily
and forget.

AFTER WATCHING THE SPACE SHUTTLE EXPLODE

In darkness, we watch movie wolves
slashing each other with fangs
bared against the moon of winter. Alone
even in family tribes, living on air,

we cast our fortunes to the stars
like sins we've tried to leave behind
in a dumpster. We confess we are beasts
without souls, we are game

no matter how many nights we lie
resolved to evolve, to make the world
obey us, to be good at last,
always a breath away from death,

that black envelope
of a universe expanding
forever beyond us. We lie alone
cursing the dark causes

that kill us. We believe we have only
each other. Even wolves fear death,
traveling and killing in packs
of other wolves they hate.

FAITH IS A RADICAL MASTER

We touch you one by one and mumble,
words stumbling on our tongues,
stunned in your blurred living room

hours after your lab report:
a little lump, a mass of bulged,
malignant cells. Telephoned,

we've come to hold you. The ghost
who walked with mourners to Emmaus
hovers in this room. We are mere mortals,

all. We don't know anything but this.
Who knows this winter drought will last?
Who swears the last blind beggar's

doomed, no spittle for his lids?
Who calls down fire from heaven
and isn't seared?

GREAT EXPECTATIONS

From the day you bring him to the nursery
you nourish him with love. He is now your child.

    You find his door locked. For the first time
    he does not let you in. You wait, knocking, then

You rise sleepily but patient when he cries,
and dream, holding him in your arms, of taking long

    open the lock with your knife. You find him reeling,
    the room putrid with fumes, his eyebrows cheek and nose

tiring hikes in the woods with him light on your back,
letting him learn early the smell of pine,

    plastered with glue. You grab him as he falls
    and lay him down, open the windows and see

the green wonder of trees. Nightly, when he is fed
and burped and heavily asleep again, you place

    the crumpled tube drooling on the bed. Later, you listen
    and talk of danger. And he lies back in tears.

the empty bottle on the floor, lay him in the crib clean
as a forest and watch him dreaming, his face peaceful

    Weeks pass. You smell the storeroom reeking of gasoline.
    Inside, you find him squatting in the dark, his mind speeding

as a fawn. You rise early to hold him awhile before work,
his mouth sucking, his bright eyes studying you.

    so fast he cannot answer you. Over the months new friends
    start dropping by, slack-shouldered, thin, their eyes

For his first birthday you invite friends who arrive
with children of their own, eager for parties.

    ancient as snakes. By thirteen, in a rage, eyeballs
    bitter as acid, he beats you with his fists

Your son, already waddling for months,
carries the torn paper and the toy. He runs

    and for the third time runs away. You chase him
    down the block until he loses you.

and falls, pushes himself up with both clutched
tightly in his fists. You take pictures by the roll.

    Searching everywhere, you place desperate ads
    in the lost and found of distant papers.

4.
Dawn of the Bitter Blizzard

WE WILL ALL LIVE ON THE PLAINS

The earth is never flat enough.
All rain drains east or west.
Even the Rockies wash down
to the plains. A decade of clouds
can start a canyon.
Men in dump trucks labor all year
filling nothing but potholes,

bulldozers mashing road shoulders
flat, along all highways
piles of macadam waiting to be crushed.
We dredge salt marshes for cities
and haul tons of rocks for foundations.
Even the sky falls, sprinkling stars
like sand over swamps.

Graves settle after rains, crack
and collapse like earthquakes.
Men drive loaded trucks
slowly among the plots,
watching for sumps. They shovel loam
into holes like eye sockets
and tamp them smooth.

THE SKULLS THAT EAT SUCH DUST

I remember scalps of soldiers in museums,
the whites of their eyes in paintings.
These flints are from bold people
who wandered the plains for bison,

a thousand pounds of meat. Bleached canyons
were valleys a thousand years ago, a flyway
for geese and cranes. A tribe could feast
near this caliche pond. Gardens sprawled

like Eden, millions of melons. With picks
and microscopes, we find the DNA of seeds,
the bowls they stored them in. They willed their skulls
to buzzards, leaving their grief to coyotes.

Blown sand buried their tongues, no names,
not even a stone. The skulls that eat such dust
are singing: at last, people to love them.
We brush their eyes with bristles,

our fingers learning to caress skeletons.
Here, they planted what we reap, a legend
of plains people under siege, never enough time
to find whatever they needed—an endless flow

of bison, the meaning of darkness, the hope
of living another night on the earth
and others to hold them. What did they do
under the onslaught of old age,

their faith in failing gods? We sift the sand
for clues, exposing only weapons.
We scrape a decade away each day,
but the moon is up, and rushing.

WHERE SKIES ARE NOT CLOUDY ALL DAY

I hear old heartache often on the plains.
The whine of steel guitars
and songs of lonely blondes escape
from pickup windows passing by.
Whoever's driving waves, and I wave back.

My dogs trot out to ask if I'm all right,
wagging their lazy tails. They're blinking
from the barn, squinting in sunlight
to prove they're loyal dogs. They wet a stalk
and trot away to nothing but shade and daydreams.

Watching a hawk, I hear another whine of tires.
Soon I'll hear the song, the same old fiddles
sobbing in a neighbor's truck, some singer
swearing a stranger's arms are all she owns,
pleading as if these plains are all she needs.

DOG-DAY AFTERNOON

Cicadas buzz and stumble
from the trees, fly slow
and lumber toward the fence.
The tom cat slashes wildly,

tail flick-flicking.
The one he stuns
lies twitching in the grass.
The dog lies panting. The cat

strolls back, a swagger,
slit eyes like jade. August
paints all colors bright,
the cat dark as an otter: sniffs,

paws as if he means to play,
nips one wing like a kitten's nape,
jogs to the gate, leaps up
and disappears.

THE SOUTHERN BROWN RECLUSE

Anything hidden is suspect—
borders of curtains
never opened behind the dresser,
caverns of old clothes,

toes of summer shoes
back in the dark, forgotten.
Formal in a brown-velvet body,
it bears a white guitar on its back,

its only music. In terror of light,
it stings anything exposed—
ankles invading closets,
hands gathering garments for charity

or probing for lost coins. Its venom
rots the skin. Only at night
will it crawl out, long crab-legs
feeling familiar carpet

like a beach littered with shells
of crickets and silverfish.
Whatever it stalks
will burn twitching,

paralyzed, a string
of live meat like a trot line.
Later, while the sun
glows through curtains,

it drags its catch
back to the secret fabrics,
reclusive and famished.
All the dark day,

its legs caress each victim
turned to jelly, even the bones,
and then it bends down
its straw tongue like a kiss.

FOLLOWING INSTINCT AND CACTUS

A prairie wears scuffed leather gloves
in public, hard to know with a handshake.
Without a cloud, we squint to see it,
heads bowed under our Stetsons,

following instinct and cactus
more than trails. A prairie never tells us
how to live under the sun,
without effort. Morning brings dark wings

and leaves them circling down range.
My wife plays mercy with her eyes
and mounts beside me, trading a known corral
for clues. I've seen her hold a skull,

puzzling the buzzards. They know the signs
of drought, the flesh that feeds them:
if this is how it ends, why worry?
They spiral a thousand yards downwind,

a wide, slow funnel above arroyos.
It's happened before—calves
that wandered off, bone-snapped
and bawling, steers too fat to climb,

too dumb to know the way around a range
where they were born, or maybe a coyote
that died howling last night,
the moon not enough for answers.

FATHER'S SHOTGUN

I lift it cold and blue, old metal
forged in Sheffield. I snap the lever,
exposing both chambers of barrels. Not a streak,
not one fine grain in either bore.
My father loved this gun, his first indulgence,
dirt-poor in the Texas depression.
I remember its heft when he let me hold it.

I staggered, too much for my two arms to aim.
Fist on my head, he steadied the stock and pointed.
"That cactus. Blow it away." I squeezed,
and needles exploded in my mind, only a click
of the trigger, the gun not loaded,
wasting no money for shells. For years
he hunted fields around our house, coyotes,

unlucky rabbits. I could count the times
that gun went off, explosions rare as thunder.
Neighbors miles away kept score, no doubt,
another of Oscar's quarters wasted.
Retired, enough social security for toothpaste,
he made me swear I'd keep it oiled

and out of reach of grandkids. I run the rod
with oil-tipped cloth both ways,
wipe both barrels clean and snap it shut,
and buff it. Zipped in the case, it's harmless
on my lap. My palms easily heft it,
like guessing the weight of a gift wrapped to mail,
no forwarding address, no way to send it.

BLACK GRANITE BURNS LIKE ICE

Watching the world from above,
all fallen friends applaud
in blisters on our backs.
Wherever I go, there's fire.

My dreams are napalm.
I've been to the wall
and placed my fingers on their names.
Black granite burns like ice

no lips can taste. Sad music's
on my mind, a war on every channel.
After the madness of Saigon
I flew back through San Francisco

to the plains, flat fields with cactus
and the ghosts of rattlers.
I feed the hawks field mice and rabbits.
I'm no Saint Francis

but even the buzzards circle,
hoping whatever I own keeps dying.
My wife's green eyes count cattle
all week long, saving each calf,

each wounded goat ripped open
by barbed wire. After dark
we rock on the porch
and watch the stars,

wondering how many owls dive
at night per acre, how many snakes
per grandchild, how many wars
before all dreams are fire.

RELEASING THE HAWK IN AUGUST

Say something sober to a hawk
and he'll rise flapping, curved talons
ready to tear your heart out.
He had that stare
the scalding day we found him

by a cactus, wing drooped,
bruised by a hunter.
After weeks of feeding him
giblets and mice he snatched
with curved beak and ripped,

we knew we'd never be friends
up close, too much alike,
his wound the temporary warp
of nature, the shape of genes,
his way of saying save me.

DAWN OF THE BITTER BLIZZARD

Bulky in coats,
we entered a world below zero
in flurries blinding us again.
Ghosts swerved on the snow

and sunlight slanted on diamonds.
Our boots crushed the stubble
of stiff alfalfa. Hard wind
ripped shingles loose, clatter of tin

on the pump house. Buzzards
perched on the power lines,
watching the dogs plow snow
with muzzles. After the last cows

staggered to the corral,
we dumped hay bales to save them,
trusting their bells to keep ringing
in stiff winds banging the roof.

WAR IN THE PERSIAN GULF

I thought I knew those wild blue skies by heart,
riding a maze of dials and switches I could touch
with my eyes closed. My fingertips aimed wings
and throttles a mile over mountains,

the seat of my pants growing numb with wisdom.
Pilot training was easy, no war, no madness anywhere.
Looping the clouds, we practiced dog fights,
scissor-turns over fields we buzzed,

scattering fat southern cattle, rich Georgia loam
black as the rims of our goggles. Who ever had such friends,
all of us drunk on wings and G-suits, Mach-1 the goal
we yearned for. What did we know, brought up on Mustangs

and Lightnings, old planes in black-and-white war movies,
silk scarfs and goggles, a band of brothers in skies
wholly for heroes—forty of us from Texas
to Boston, ten from South America,

three handsome swarthy boys from Iraq.
I've read accounts in Air Force magazines.
One of us rode to the moon and back. One died
in the Georgia loam, others over Hanoi or Laos,

four wore stars, retired, kicked back in Lazy Boys
watching the news, counting beads or dozing,
cursing the war or praying, awed by jets
we never flew, stealth-fighter routes

in desert skies. I try to recall those other boys
in Georgia and wonder where they are,
watching TV for close-ups of Iraqi soldiers,
hoping I'll recognize them, hoping I won't.

5.
Across Dark Fields of Coyotes

WHATEVER OUR FISTS FIND

No other boats, a mile from shore.
My sons click penlights off and on
like code, grown men on a harbor of water.
I close the throttle. Far under us

lunkers cruise deep troughs.
We gild our hooks with sunfish filets
smooth as suede, splash them over the side
and count. Invisible lines snick out

down to mad bass needing no moon,
no fragile boat to support them. Bobbing,
we brace for whatever our fists find
leaping and dying at midnight.

THE BARN ON THE BRAZOS

The hasp is off, the padlock missing.
Even the anvil's gone, nothing on pegs
but rotten hames of horses. We thought all owls
were dead until we saw their modest droppings,
dry tangles of fur and bones.

I don't blame anonymous neighbors for plunder
I've ignored. Here, Grandpa pounded on mustangs,
filing their hooves, fitting the cooled shoes
and sinking the beveled nails, his hammer swung
by a bicep hugely bulged. When I touched that arm

my fingers couldn't reach. I rose on his arm
toward heaven. Even now, I can hear the clang
of steel on the anvil, the forge like Satan's gullet.
I thought nothing could ever be that hot again.
I've been to Saigon and back. Banging

clangs in the rafters overhead, the pop and groan
of old planks held by nails he drove.
The dust has settled, no motes of straw
or specks of horse dung floating in our lungs.
Even the owls don't bother to ask us who.

They've held their breath so long
another hour won't kill them,
not if we'll close the door behind us.
Whatever they hunt comes out at night, scurries
across the straw, the splatter of sand.

My knees and old boots creak as I bend
to pick up nails. My wife doesn't laugh
at my cocked ear, tuned for the clang of steel,
the puff and sizzle of an iron shoe doused,
something to last until a work horse threw it,

lost forever in weeds, unless some boy
with a cane pole on his shoulder found
and cleaned the shoe with his hand, spat on it
for luck and tossed it over his head
behind him, not looking back.

A THOUSAND YARDS DOWNHILL

Embers blaze back nights of bonfires
ice can't echo. Wild nights
when our children skied
linger in blinks of slides
fierce light projects.

A river tumbles underground
and comes back up for air
a thousand yards downhill. Foam
is its only note, it holds it all day,
gushing up from that deep cave

and babbling resurrection.
When we backpack halfway between eagle
and otter, we never climb the same trail
twice, sliding on shale each step,
the eyes of all things wild

straining to see who's here.
Our married children sleep
in distant condominiums, skiing
when it snows enough for powder
deep as dreams we cling to

these slow nights, enough for two-log fires
to rock by, hours after we hoped
long-distance phones would ring, Hello,
Hello? Even in this cabin we're not alone.
This calm would be screams

to a stethoscope, gongs
to the inner ear. Think of the softest
saxophone note you've ever heard,
diminuendo. For now
let silence be enough.

ALL THE OLD SONGS

I never knew them all, just hummed
and thrummed my fingers with the radio,
driving a thousand miles to Austin.
Her arms held all the songs I needed.
Our boots kept time with fiddles
and the charming sobs of blondes,

the whine of steel guitars
sliding us down in deer-hide chairs
when jukebox music was over.
Sad music's on my mind tonight
in a jet high over Dallas, earphones
on channel five. A lonely singer,

dead, comes back to beg me,
swearing in my ears she's mine,
rhymes set to music which make
complaints seem true. She's gone
and others like her, leaving their songs
to haunt us. Letting down through clouds

I know who I'll find tonight at home,
the same woman faithful to my arms
as she was those nights in Austin
when the world seemed like a jukebox,
our boots able to dance forever,
our pockets full of coins.

SOMETHING SIMPLE LIKE THE WEATHER

I let these babies crawl my arms and scalp,
help the toddler ride my horsey foot
until it drops. "Pop!" the toddler shouts.
I am her cloud to bounce on, the doting
grandfather I always wanted. I see our children
in these children's lips and eyes. I never
make the same mistakes, if I'm able.

We survived the summer storms, the wise
tornado warnings. I forget what we wanted
on those unwary days, too busy sorting diapers
from desire. It was all we could do
to put our simple house in order—
four parents dead before we knew them,
our children clawing to grow up.

I take my time, this time, a harmless,
kind old visitor, a bottomless pocket of toys
and sugarless bubble gum. Without the aid
of wrinkles and weather maps, how could I grasp
something simple like children's toys,
the mystery of rain, the stalled squall lines,
the wide, clear shots from space?

MEMORIAL DAY

I like old soldiers on parade.
Whatever they did or didn't do,
it's over. Bricks are reasons
for living, drums beating time

for boots and khaki pants that fit—
years after war, a reason to welcome
growing old, something to count on,
medals to wear in public,

heads high as arthritis allows
and stories almost forgotten.
Whatever we won't tell others
we tell ourselves at night,

rocking in chairs when sleep
like a prisoner of war escapes,
leaving us here on the home front
with dreams tattered like flags,

no weapons to lock and load,
only trick knees and knuckles stiff,
eyes that won't focus
without glasses we grab for

when something taps us awake,
our turn on watch, the enemy sighted
out there in jungles,
outnumbered, but coming.

HOMECOMING, CLASS OF '52

We toasted old friends' wives with the clink
of brown bottles held aloft. We rose
and touched their ribs for luck, the dance floor
almost deserted. Stunned to see so many of us home,

we laughed about old times and crossed the room
with the rhythm, jukebox caught on three sweet
bitter beats. When scratchy records ended,
we led them back to their husbands,

paunchy, balding strangers disguised as friends.
We didn't believe the stars we followed
would lead us back worn-out so soon,
years after Korea and the death of classmates.

But there we sat, swapping lies and bragging
that most of it never came true,
not even atomic wars Mr. Roades foretold
in Physics. How few we saw today, old teachers

we thought were ancient then, but only our age
now, we realized, cold sober on beer
and our women's menopause, our hernias
and prostates news we paraded like battle scars.

IN GUSTY WINDS THIS WILD

Lakes ankle-deep are lacquered with sand
all spring. Hoisting a fat black bass,
I see it flip and splash the surface.
Deer flashing their flags are nervous,

trusting no odor in gusty winds this wild.
Cattle outlast the wind by fasting,
huddled as if asleep. I might as well
raise moles and gophers as cows.

Coyotes that claim our fields
cough, clearing their throats. The moon
is a lozenge they swallow, head back
and howling. Later, they slink off

under stars. Dogs are worthless in sandstorms.
They blink, sleeping all day when they can.
Mornings, we find them covered. They rise
and shake sprays of gold dust in our faces.

We bend down and pat them, puffs of smoke
as if burning. Whatever we touch is dust.
Sand grits on the porch like saddles
stretched and creaking. At noon,

we rock on the screened porch,
breathing the dust we're made of,
rinsing our mouths with coffee.
We like the calm, dazzled hour of sundown,

no wind, mystery enough to hear each other,
the noise of whispers, the only other sound
the groaning porch swing chains
anchored above us, gliding over and over.

WHEN THE CIRCUS IS OVER

We come back bored, too many seconds
  on the clock, a thousand clowns
    and not one laugh. If children

of all ages scream, then what are we?
  Cotton candy still melts sticky
    in our fists. Say something young:

the grandkids. Right away
  we're smiling sticky smiles
    at all we meet. They would have loved

the lions with men caught
  bowing in their throats. Trapeze
    and elephant acts come back

to haunt us with applause. We flip
  through the program, half the acts
    no longer with the circus,

but believing what we read,
  needing another cannon
    firing live girls at the net.

IN THE HIBISCUS GARDEN

Even his wagging tail can bring us to our knees.
We feed him chicken bits and watch his tongue
take in whatever we can give. He flicks his eyes
between us, accepts what each hand offers.
Fifteen's a long time for a dog. We look away

and squeeze the greasy giblets. Red oaks
no older than this dog keep us in shade.
Our busy hands can't let him go. He shoves
to lift himself, leans to make the trembling world
stand still, and wobbles to the round steel bowl.

THE LAST GOOD SADDLES

We've worked these plains so long we're broke.
Two old neighbors can't make the dust feed calves
forever. August this hot makes yucca
drop its pods, snakes hibernate till dark,

horned owls believe they're wise,
grasping the limbs of live oaks.
Black buzzards glide, patrolling all we own.
Wherever they swirl, coyotes are sure to follow,

starving for cow bones broken,
tumbled down steep arroyos. Soon,
we'll round up strays enough to drive
to two corrals, brands on their flanks

better than fences to keep two fools
from quarrels—this calf is mine,
that, yours, the brittle grass they find
on open range good to be chewed over and over.

Rolling a smoke the old way, we listen to thunder,
the distant rumble of rain. Too late
to do much good this season even if it floods.
You spit, and wipe a stiff glove over stubble.

Buzzards seem fatter than these steers.
But let's go, coaxing our sorrels back
between mesquite and cactus, the simple oats
they work for at least enough for them.

Tonight at the campfire we'll sip cold beer
and quarrel about taxes and the price of bulls,
about drought and stalled squall lines,
about whose old bones first felt the rain.

"HOW DID I GET SO OLD?"

The school bell beckons
and they come with books
and kindergarten smiles,

running before they know it
up the stage steps
for diplomas,

some stumbling into money
and love and marriage,
some stumbling

into foxholes and body bags,
most stumbling into bed
with stiff knees

and gingivitised gums
of mouths too old to learn new words,
to answer the bell.

A STROLL AROUND THE DANCE FLOOR

Oh, cup your hands and clap, the music's over.
Even clover honey sugars in the cold,
the hardiest bees soon food for fire ants.

Hitch up the plow and turn the mortgaged sand
to sorghum. Cows faithful to their cycles
must be fed, and bulls are only scrotums

dragged about by horns. Not all good music's
in the fiddles of tonight, no steel guitars
hold all the chords we're after. Come,

some other night we'll find them in the eyes
of friends from Amarillo, lonely like us
for a stroll around the dance floor,

a cushion of sawdust underfoot
slippery as ice, the better to hold
each other tightly and not fall.

ACROSS DARK FIELDS OF COYOTES

We scurry from town to town
across dark fields of coyotes,
measuring miles like a surveyor's chain,
thumping of tires all night

over seams of tar in the concrete,
the time of night disk jockeys love,
dark starlight perfect for fiddles
and steel guitars. The mind is a wheel

and can stall dead-still, dreaming.
More danger than on-rushing cars
is sleep, simply to drift away.
If we take turns steering

we'll meet the dawn in Dallas,
a driveway littered with toys,
grandkids to cuddle, a week of those
worth all the flat miles home.